RORY GREEN

SECRET AGENT
TO THE
QUEEN

Kerry McIntosh

CRANTHORPE
—MILLNER—

Alfred!
Bee brilliant!
Love
Kmc x

First published by Cranthorpe Millner Publishers (2022)

ISBN 978-1-80378-057-3 (Paperback)

www.cranthorpemillner.com

Cranthorpe Millner Publishers

For all my family and friends, some passed, but all present. I'm so grateful for your continuing love and guidance. This book is for you and because of you. I love you x

Chapter One

The sunlight highlighted Rory's mop of ginger hair, and his tongue glistened, poking out of the corner of his mouth as he concentrated. He was staring at his laptop, cutting and pasting an article about deforestation into his school project entitled, 'How We Can All Play a Part in Saving the Planet'. Suddenly, a little bee wafted through the window and loomed large as it buzzed around his head, making him jump.

"Get off me, silly bee," he begged.

As he leapt out of its way, he narrowly missed colliding with his perfect Lego replica of Batman's Batcave, which he and his late Grandad Bobbee had spent hours and hours lovingly constructing on Rory's last birthday. Rory's mum's voice echoed up the stairs.

"Rory! I'm going to count to five, and if you're not by the front door with your shoes neatly tied, ready to go, I will take that laptop away from you and we won't be going anywhere."

Rory sighed. He picked up his very favourite Lego and placed it carefully on the shelf that his dad had put up above his desk for all his creations. Then he took the telescopic arm he had made out of toilet roll cardboard from beside his desk, and used it to reach a piece of paper from his recycled paper tray. This tray sat neatly between the recycled can tray and the recycled plastic tray, in a special drawer unit that he had received for his birthday, which he had positioned just beneath the window. It was neatly labelled, using different coloured card from the boxes of his favourite breakfast cereals, cut out with scissors. He used the paper to shoo the bee out of his open window and closed the window firmly behind it. He then packed away his laptop into his red backpack and collected it from his bed, before making his way along the landing.

"I don't want to go to the stupid caravan park," he groaned to himself, as he stomped down the stairs like a moody elephant towards his mum, who stood with one hand on the wall by the front door, trying to be patient.

"Come on Ploddington. Quickly. It will do you good to get away from the city air and into nature for a while."

"Being in nature makes me nervous," Rory complained, as he reached the bottom of the stairs and looked up at his mum. "All those unpredictable insects... and animals that just appear out of nowhere."

"Now what would Grandad Bobbee say to that?" she asked, teasing.

"It'll put hairs on your chest, kid," they said in unison with a big smile.

Rory's mum looked up and away so that Rory couldn't see her lip quivering as she remembered Grandad.

"Grandad Bobbee would have been so happy that we are taking this trip in his memory," she said as her eyes filled with salty tears. "He loved taking us there when we were your age. I know it isn't exactly your thing, but please try and make the most of it," she pleaded as she pointed to the front door. "Pop your things in the caravan," she smiled, as he passed her and left through the front door.

Rory stepped inside the caravan for the first time, with his mum behind him. He drank it all in. The cushions surrounding the brown dining table were brown. The kitchen cabinets above and below the brown worktop were also brown. The carpet that ran from the brown wooden floor into the lounge area was a pale brown, but still, it was brown.

"Why is everything brown?" Rory asked.

"Brown was very trendy in Grandad Bobbee's time," Mum said, picking up a small, framed photograph from a shelf. The photograph showed Rory's family with a jolly looking Grandad Bobbee, who wore a bushy moustache nestled proudly under his nose. His glasses framed the sparkle in his eyes. She looked at the photo lovingly, brushing a finger over Grandad Bobbee's face, then carefully replaced it on the shelf.

"Let's get this show on the road then, shall we?" said Rory's dad, as he leant into the caravan holding Rory's baby sister Lucy, who was drooling all down his hairy arm.

Rory's mum ushered him out of the caravan and into the car. "You heard your dad. Let's go," she said.

Just then, the little bee that had buzzed around Rory's head earlier appeared again and swooped in towards him.

"You again? I said get off," Rory grumbled as he flapped his hands about his head anxiously. He jumped into the car and slammed the door behind him.

"Be kind, Rory. Doors have feelings too,"

joked Dad as he crunched the car into gear and heaved the prehistoric caravan off the driveway. Rory smirked as he caught his dad's eye in the rear-view mirror.

A giant wooden sign appeared on the left of the roadside, emblazoned with the words 'Welcome to The Great Oaks Campsite', as Dad turned down a gravel driveway.

Rory wondered what made their oak trees so great. The campsite owner, Farmer Frank, an elderly man in green corduroy trousers and a checked shirt, directed them to an available pitch. As the car stopped, a black and white dog circled around it like it was a sheep to be rounded up. Mum got out of the car like a giddy schoolgirl, excited to be there. But her excitement was quickly squashed once she saw her once beloved forest all dark and bare.

"Farmer Frank, what on Earth happened?" she asked as she walked towards him. "The trees look so sad. And where are the bluebells? They were Dad's favourite."

"It's quite dreadful, I know. A strange pink fungus has taken hold of the entire forest. I've tried to get rid of it, but it won't give up for anything. It's taken over, and nobody is booking to stay with us, or visiting the forest, or buying produce from the local farms. It's a complete disaster for the forest but also our livelihoods."

Rory unhooked his seatbelt and jumped out. Ahead of him was what seemed like a wall of rotten wood. His gaze followed the wall to the left, then to the right, and then he looked up. And up. And up. A. Great. Big.

Rotten. Oak tree! With dozens more rotting beside it.

"Woah," said Rory, shocked. .

"We used to hold the world record for the biggest oak trees in the world," Farmer Frank explained. "But now they are rotting from the outside in. In their heyday they were each around one hundred and four feet tall, and their trunks fifty feet around. A couple of them are still standing strong. Rory, I can show you how to climb them later if you want?"

"Oh, err... no... no thanks. I'm okay," said Rory sheepishly.

Rory's mum smiled and ruffled his hair knowingly. "He prefers to read about nature rather than get his hands dirty."

"Why would you want to get your hands dirty? Nearly eighty percent of illness-causing germs are spread by your hands," said Rory, matter-of-factly.

"You're not as adventurous as your mum was when she was a kiddy then?" guessed Farmer Frank.

"Not at all adventurous, no," said Rory's mum as she sank into the farmer's hug. "Lovely to see you again Frank. Dad would've loved to be with us."

"You too, pet. You go and get yourselves settled and we'll reminisce about your dad later. We were such good friends."

"Sounds good," she said.

Later that day, whilst Mum, Dad and Lucy joined Farmer Frank for a cup of tea and a biscuit, Rory watched out of the caravan window so closely that his breath steamed up the glass. A group of children, armed with paintball guns, had surrounded a red squirrel as it minded its own business, foraging for food on the barren forest floor.

"Aim," said Travis, the ringleader, to his crew.

Rory tapped on the window so timidly that it could have been a tickle, and of course, nobody heard.

"Fire!" yelled Travis as if he was heading for war.

Rory banged on the window with such gusto that not only did he scare himself, but the squirrel stood up on its hind legs in a frenzied panic and scurried away from the commotion. Travis had a face like thunder and turned to point his paintball gun at the caravan, just as Rory ducked down, hoping not to be spotted. But the steamed glass, with nostril shaped holes, could still be seen, as could the shocking blur of Rory's red hair.

"Oi ginger kid," Travis yelled as he and his friends hurtled towards Rory in their wellington boots, which made funny fart noises as they ran. They sounded hilarious, but right now, Rory felt scared. He curled into a ball as Travis and his friends tried to rock the caravan from side to side, making it sway like an old pirate ship on stormy seas. All the furniture and the pots and pans rattled. Hugging his knees into his chest and tucking his head in so that he didn't get hurt, each rock of the caravan rolled Rory around like he was inside a pinball machine. He pinged from the brown sofa to the brown bean bag, and then to the brown table and along the brown wooden floor until he pinged off the brown kitchen unit and rolled out of the open door onto the grass.

"Get him!" yelled Travis.

Without hesitation Rory jumped to his feet and circled the campsite. He ran around every empty caravan, every available tent pitch, the deathly quiet launderette, the desolate grocery store, and then pegged it into the rotten forest. He weaved in and out of the rotten oak trees, trying to not be seen. As they lost sight of him, the bullies slowed.

"Where did he go?" asked Travis, trying to catch his breath.

The other boys shrugged their shoulders as they bent over, puffing and panting. The forest was still once more.

Chapter Two

Meanwhile, high in the canopy of one of the rotten oak trees, Queen Bee looked through her regal glasses and down her regal nose at the chaos and commotion of the Annual Bee Conference. Thousands of bees, young and old, buzzed around the magnificent Beehive Stadium, nestled within Queen Bee's hive.

Bobbee, a cuddly, bumbly old bee, who had a bushy moustache and a sparkle in his eye, stood in a long queue of bees. He popped his head to the side and looked down the long line that snaked to the front of the auditorium, wondering if he would ever get to the front. It was fascinating to watch as the bee at the front of the queue was spun like candyfloss at the fair. When Bobbee reached the front, he was pulled and prodded as machines collected the visual data that his visor had collected on expedition. Then, a giant hoover sucked up the cotton-wool-like pollen from Bobbee's fluffy black and gold body. For a moment, he looked up, dazzled by the marvelousness of the pollen as it moved through a transparent pipe into a giant computer, before he was cast aside.

"Settle bees, settle," said Queen Bee loudly from a freestanding microphone at the centre of the stage.

The microphone failed to amplify her voice and the chaos continued. The show runner quickly set Queen Bee up with a head microphone, which she enjoyed immensely.

"Oh, I feel like Bee-yoncé," she said excitedly, which finally caught the bees' attention.

They all shuffled their bee bottoms down, and a giant screen at the front of the auditorium lit up, flashing image after image of hundreds of children's faces. Bobbee tried to focus but the faces passed so quickly that they sort of blurred into each other, making them completely unrecognisable. Suddenly, the screen froze, and you could hear a bee-sting drop as the entire auditorium stopped to consider the image. But only one bee would recognise it.

"To whom does this child belong?" asked Queen Bee expectantly.

The entire audience raised their hands, except for Bobbee, who couldn't believe his eyes.

16

"I'm not looking for a wanna-bee, but the actual bee-guardian of this child", she said.

With that, all bees put down their hands with a hurumph, and Queen Bee pulled out a print-out from the giant computer.

"This computer reading shows that this child matches ninety-nine per cent of the qualities required for my special agent's role, which is quite wonderful. Does *anyone* know this child?" Her question was met with silence. "Anyone?"

Bobbee stared at the image in disbelief. Queen Bee glared across at her show runner, who then handed her a gold card. She looked through her glasses, then back up to the audience.

"His name is Rory Green!" she hollered, her voice echoing throughout the stadium and finally penetrating Bobbee's ears. He started to feel a little faint as she yelled again. "Is this microphone even working?" She tapped it forcefully and yelled again. "Rory! Green!"

Bobbee looked around at the other bees, convinced it couldn't be his Rory, but nobody moved. In a moment of clarity, Bobbee bounced out of his seat as if he had won the lottery.

"Y-y-y-y-yes, ma'am. That's my boy, Rory." A spotlight hit his face, dazzling him, and a fanfare sounded which made the entire audience erupt.

"Thank goodness. Let's give him a huge bee conference congratulations then!" Queen Bee buzzed as she looked out across the sea of bees, who were all beside themselves with excitement, buzzing and shouting, whooping and clapping.

Bobbee lifted his chin and his shoulders relaxed back. He felt sort of important.

"Please join us on stage so that we can see

why your boy has been selected to be my special agent," said Queen Bee.

Bobbee buzzed down the stadium steps in shock, but he smiled and greeted the other bees' grins and stares. He felt like a local celebrity as cameras flashed in his face and he joined Queen Bee at the side of the stage. The lights darkened dramatically in the auditorium and a spotlight lit the screen as the footage captured by Bobbee showed Rory clinging to the branches of a giant oak tree, still hiding from Travis, and completely out of breath.

"The information collected on your expedition shows that Rory is a highly intelligent and compassionate child, who is certainly an excellent runner. Where is the boy now?"

"Still up the tree, ma'am," said Bobbee.

"Bring him to me," said Queen Bee.

"Yes ma'am, it would be an honour," he
replied. Bobbee remained still as he looked

out into the audience, still taken aback by the experience. Queen Bee cleared her throat to get his attention. He looked at her and melted at her authority.

"Oh, right now?"

"Yes, go now. I will expect you both at my hivequarters by nightfall," she said.

"Right-o. I mean, of course ma'am. I'll get straight to it," he replied as he buzzed straight off the stage, greeted by high-fives, pats on the back, and requests for autographs by the other bees lining his exit. He zipped out of the door with a sense of duty and pride in his heart and a big smile on his face.

Back in the forest of rotten oak trees at the

bottom of 'Great Oaks' campsite, the air was full of a funky kind of smell. Bobbee buzzed around Rory's head as he held on tightly to a tree branch, still hiding out from Travis and his friends. Rory tried to swat him away like an angry ninja.

"Get away you bee. Camping is rubbish and stupid and way worse than being at home." Rory didn't like bees, or green grass, or giant trees. "I said, go away," said Rory, wobbling on his branch as he swung his arms around again to try and shoo Bobbee away.

A woodpecker buried its beak into the rotting wood next to him and started pecking at it like a mini battering ram, which made Rory wobble more. He was terrified of woodpeckers. He reached out his hands, which were starting to go a little white from his tight grip, and suddenly the blood rushed back to them, before disappearing down his veins again as he found a better branch to cling to. A fat, feathery pigeon, one of his most feared birds, landed on his branch, making him jump out of his skin, lose his grip, and fall like a sack of potatoes onto the ground.

Ouch!

Rory's body hurt all over. He daren't look in case he had broken into a million pieces, so he kept his eyes firmly shut. All he could hear was the little bee buzzing around him, until a very familiar voice spoke directly into his ear.

"Rory? Rory? Are you okay? Where does it hurt?" Bobbee fussed.

"Grandad?" groaned Rory, puzzled.

"The very same," said Bobbee who was pleased as punch to be reunited with his grandson.

Rory sat up and opened his eyes wide like it was Christmas morning. He looked around

for his cuddly and energetic grandad, but all
he could see was the still and sad looking
forest around him.

"Down here," said Bobbee as he landed on the end of Rory's nose. "You like my new black and gold threads?" he said, twirling to show off his bee stripes.

Rory went cross-eyed as he tried to focus on the noise coming from his nose, but for the first time he showed no fear.

"Grandad, is that you?" asked Rory, looking puzzled.

"Yes, it's me, kid! I promise it is," said Bobbee.

"My grandad wasn't a bee though," said Rory, not understanding a thing.

"I know, but I'm still your grandad. I can prove it. Ask me anything."

"Hmm, my brain hurts a little, but okay... what was my grandad's favourite sweet?" asked Rory.

Bobbee buzzed away from Rory's nose, doing a loop-the-loop excitedly. "Easy!

Humbugs! And still is!"

Rory wasn't really sure how this strange little bee could know that, so he hit him again with a quickfire round of inquisition.

"Favourite hobby?"

"Gardening."

"Favourite garden tool."

"Not a tool really, but the ride-on mower was the most fun!"

"It really was," Rory replied wistfully, remembering the days when they had raced around the garden both astride it, with Grandad at the wheel hugging him in tightly. He shook himself.

"Okay, this will get you. How many lights did my grandad put up around the garden shed and why?" Rory glared at the bee, knowing that he had stumped him this time.

"Seventy-eight," said Bobbee. "My age at the time." Rory's eyes and his mouth widened, not believing it as Bobbee continued. "You told me that Father Christmas wouldn't see our house unless I created a runway of lights for his sleigh to descend into the garden."

Rory couldn't understand it but paused at the familiar bushy moustache and trademark sparkle in the bee's eyes. Then it hit him. His face lit up.

"Grandad! You are a bee!" Rory swept him up towards his cheek with his hand and gave him a squishy, loving sort-of hug. "I've missed you so much. What are you doing here? Mum said you were climbing trees in heaven."

"I was sort of doing something very close to that kid," said Grandad.

"But bees don't talk," said Rory.

"They do. But you're the only human that can hear me because I'm your bee-buddy," said Bobbee.

"I don't understand," said Rory.

"I will try and explain. When I was poorly, I could never have imagined that after I left this world I would be given such a wonderful new opportunity. I expected to put my feet up and get a well-earned rest, but instead, they gave me a new job. As a bee! As it turns out us bees are very important. We get to use our life experience from the time we were on Earth as humans to make sure that you, the world's children, protect the future of our planet. I was ushered into the bee world and tasked with looking after you," he said. "Isn't that something?"

"That's not just something, Grandad, that's epic! So we get to hang out again like we used to? Build Lego and eat humbugs?" asked Rory excitedly.

"We definitely get to hang out. But there's also something very important that I need to ask you, by order of Her Majesty Queen Bee," he said.

"Awesome, I can't wait. We can watch nature documentaries all day long and—" Rory suddenly stopped talking as the enormity of what his grandad had said hit him. "Wait? What? The queen bee wants to ask *me* something? Why me? She doesn't know me," said Rory, flustered.

"Every year, the bee conference votes for an environmental issue to be prioritised. But this year, Her Majesty decided that instead of us focusing on an environmental issue, a child needed to be selected to become her human secret agent. Of course, it couldn't be just anyone; the data we have collected over the years had to be thoroughly analysed to find the right person for the job."

"What data, Grandad?" asked Rory, keen to know more details.

"Every moment that we spend buzzing around you, audio and visual impressions are taken, which are downloaded into the pollen that we collect, and it is that data which is analysed.

"How clever," said Rory.

"Very clever," said Bobbee. "And at today's annual conference, the bees voted, and the collected pollen was analysed, and a child was chosen to be Queen Bee's secret agent."

"Amazing. Well good luck to her, or him. Let me know how they get on won't you?"

Bobbee pulled out a computer printout from his black and gold bee backpack and unfurled it.

"This printout is your bee report card. It shows a percentage score of how closely you have matched the requirements." Bobbee handed Rory the piece of paper which read

'99% match'. Rory glanced at it:

1.   Courageous
2.   Inventive
3.   Kind
4.   Compassionate
5.   Cares about the environment

Rory looked puzzled.

"It's you Rory. You're the chosen child."

Rory handed the report card straight back dismissively. "It only says a ninety-nine percent match, so it can't be me," said Rory with relief.

"Nobody is perfect," said Bobbee, "but you were by far the most highly scored kid."

Rory thought for a moment. "What is the role of this secret agent anyway?" he asked.

"To undertake missions to protect the environment by order of Her Majesty, and make sure the natural world is safe," said Bobbee.

"But I could never do that. I'm just a kid," said Rory.

"How do you know unless you try?" said Bobbee.

Rory fell silent as he thought carefully.

"To accept the position, you must report for duty to Queen Bee before nightfall," said Bobbee.

"Hmm..." Rory fell silent again, not knowing what to say.

"Just think about it, okay?" said Bobbee. Rory nodded reluctantly and Bobbee buzzed off.

Chapter Three

Later, Rory appeared from the dark and dingy forest, and kicked up the dead spring leaves that the fungus had forced to the ground. He had thought long and hard about what Bobbee had asked him.

"Lunch time Rory," called his mum from the caravan.

He climbed the steps with a *thud thud thud* as if he had the weight of the world on his shoulders. Before he could put his foot down inside, his mum stopped him in his tracks.

"Uh, uh, shoes off."

Rory didn't understand why he should need to take his shoes off. There was a sort of musty old boot smell in the caravan and everything was brown anyway.

"Can you set the table please?" his mum asked.

Rory obediently wandered to the brown kitchen drawer, shaking with anxiety, and pulled out four placemats, three forks, three knives, and a sort of bendy plastic spoon for Lucy. She didn't really use the spoon but liked to push things around on her plate or comb her hair with it.

"Are you okay?" asked Rory's mum.

"I would be if we had have stayed at home," said Rory under his breath.

"You would be what?" she asked, unable to hear him beneath Lucy's gurgling.

"I'm fine. What are we having?" he said.

"Cheese and honey sandwiches," said Mum.

"Okay," said Rory.

"Just okay? I thought they were your favourite?"

Of all the sandwiches, Rory would only eat the cheese and honey kind. Grandad Bobbee used to make them for him. He shrugged his shoulders.

"And salad," she added.

"Ugh," said Rory, sticking his tongue out.

Mum placed a large salad bowl of lettuce, tomato and cucumber, on the table, followed by the sandwiches.

Rory stared at the salad bowl in a daze as his dad carried Lucy to the table. She was sucking a piece of Rory's Lego, leaving sticky wet goo all over it.

"No Lucy, that's mine," Rory yelled, jumping up from his seat to grab it from her.

Rory wasn't sure how he felt about having

a sister. She cried a lot of the time. He did think it was okay having a sister sometimes, but mostly when she was asleep.

"Enough Rory. She isn't doing any harm," said Dad.

Rory's eyes glazed over.

"You aren't quite yourself, son. What's up?" asked Mum.

Rory couldn't quite articulate how he was feeling. All he knew was that he felt stuck. Really stuck.

"I'll be okay once I've eaten, I'm sure of it," he said.

"Don't just stare at it then. Eat up," said Mum.

Rory picked up the salad bowl, distracted, and took a handful of salad out and put it on his plate. Mum looked at Dad, surprised yet proud that Rory was actually going to start eating his greens finally at the age of nine.

"Well, I never thought I'd see the day," said Mum.

Rory kept piling the leaves onto his plate, until the bowl was empty.

"Come on hangry monster, leave some for the rest of us please," said Dad, now with a giant crinkling frown line on his forehead.

"I can't do it, and you can't make me," yelled Rory as he slammed down the salad bowl onto the table and ran to his bedroom. Rory's Mum and Dad looked at each other, utterly confused.

Rory buried his face into his pillow, sucking the cotton material into his mouth with each deep and frustrated breath. In and out, in and out. Suddenly he pulled his head up, the creases from the pillow etched into his cheeks, and he reached across onto the other twin bed beside and pulled his laptop from his bag. He opened the file 'How We Can All Play a Part in Saving the Planet, by Rory Green', and scrolled through each page with purpose.

Rory's freckled knees knocked together as he looked up at the giant black oak tree and Queen Bee's hive that nestled under its branch high above. The stench of the forest got up his nose.

"Achooooo!" he sneezed.

"Bless you!" said Bobbee.

"Grandad Bobbee?" he whispered. Bobbee appeared instantly on the end of his nose, excited to see him.

"I knew you'd see sense," he said.

"No, I'm afraid that I haven't seen any sense. I can't help Queen Bee. I have far too much homework to be a secret agent and—"

"You're afraid. I get it," said Bobbee.

"No, I'm not. I'm just very busy," said Rory as he turned to walk away. He was very good at walking away from things that made him worried, but mostly there was no reason for him to face his fears, so he didn't bother trying.

Bobbee reached into his bee backpack and pulled out a pair of tiny but otherwise fairly ordinary looking goggles. "Here, take a look," he said.

Rory held the tiny goggles and squinted through them using one eye. The entire landscape of the campsite through the goggles was one of nothingness. There were no longer any giant oak trees, just tree stumps where they used to be.

"How did you do that?" asked Rory, shocked at his outlook. "Those are my 'future' goggles," explained Bobbee. "All bees have a backpack full of magic gadgets. I'm not sure what all of them do just yet but I figured this one out. I just wanted to show you what could happen if the fungus is allowed to get its grip on the forest," said Bobbee.

Rory couldn't take it all in, and fell silent, wanting to disappear under a rock. Suddenly he felt drawn to his laptop bag and pulled out the bee report card curiously. He stared at the list of mission requirements again, and the analysis of his suitability, until it burned his eyes.

"But what if I fail?" asked Rory.

"Failure is just a buzz away from greatness," said Bobbee, hopeful.

Rory took a deep breath and put the bee report card back in his bag slowly and carefully, being sure not to crease it.

"I'm not sure that I am the great one that you are after, but if you really insist that I am, I will try my best."

"You are the best. That's why Queen Bee selected you," said Bobbee.

Rory took a deep breath of the country air, feeling it reach every corner of his lungs, and began to climb up the blackened trunk of the great oak tree towards Queen Bee's hivequarters. As one foot followed the other, he looked for a safe place to put his hands as he tried his best to negotiate the slimy pink fungus, which was stuck to the bark of the tree like glue. *I hope Queen Bee has some antibacterial wipes up there*, he thought.

Unintentionally, he placed his left foot on the fungus and slipped, dropping through the branches. His green hoodie took the fall as it tore over a spikey branch. He dangled, swinging like a clock pendulum.

"Help! Help!" he cried out in fear. "Grandad Bobbee, please help! I can't do this. I'm not even one percent courageous.

Bobbee buzzed alongside him, and in his best cheerleader voice, yelled his support. "You've got this kid. Just two more branches and you'll have successfully completed your climb to meet the queen."

Rory's bottom lip quivered with worry but he moved onward and upward and into motion again. Hooking a leg onto the tree he could see the hive above, hugging a nook where the bottom branch met the trunk of the gnarly tree. It was much smaller than he had imagined – about the size of his head – and certainly more rugged in real life than the pretty image on the side of a honey jar. He pulled himself up with a grimace on his face.

Resting his bottom on the branch next to the hive he tried hard not to flinch as bees darted in and out of little holes that covered the outer shell. He reached into his bag and pulled out his asthma inhaler to try and get his breathing under control. He took a puff, breathing sharply in, and deeply out again, which rejuvenated him a little. Bobbee settled on Rory's shoulder and encouraged him to breathe deeply in and out like he was head coach on the sidelines of a football match. His face looked like a pufferfish as he demonstrated the breathing technique and it made Rory giggle.

"If the wind changes, you'll stay that way

forever," chuckled Rory. Bobbee made the face again but even more exaggerated, just to make Rory laugh and relax. Grandad Bobbee always knew how to calm Rory down when he became uptight and anxious, and Rory was grateful.

At that moment, Queen Bee exited the hive through a tiny hole at the top and wafted in like she was surfing on a feather. She landed on Rory's shoulder beside Bobbee.

"What is one doing, Bobbee?" she asked as she caught him mid-inhale.

Embarrassed, Bobbee blew the air out of his cheeks and put his shoulders back. "Sorry Your Majesty, this is Rory."

"Reporting for duty," Rory said timidly.

"Your Highness," whispered Bobbee, correcting him.

"Sorry. Your Highness," said Rory as he gawped at Queen Bee. "Wow, you're a real live queen," said Rory, astonished by her beauty and sparkling crown.

"Thank you, Rory. Yes, I am a real live queen, and I'm very pleased to see you at my hive. You are a very special young man."

"I am?"

"Bee-lieve me. There are many subjects who pass through the data test for my special annual mission each year, but never have we ever had a ninety-nine percent match for our mission. You are our new secret agent," she said. "Your grandfather, Bobbee, tells me that you like nature, Rory?"

Rory's eyes opened wide and he shook his head. "No, actually I'm petrified of nature. And wildlife and bugs and just about all animals and everything really," he said hoping that maybe Queen Bee would change her mind about him.

"Well, that's rather inconvenient. But no

matter. Your first mission is to help cure the great oaks of their fungus problem and stop a development proposal that will destroy all nature and wildlife in its path," she said. "The forest is full of mature acorn producing oak trees, and without them there will be no homes for wildlife, not to mention the oxygen provided by the great oaks will be diminished. Without the oxygen produced by plants like the great oaks, humans and other animals would not be able to breathe. Did you know that it takes twenty years for an oak tree to start producing acorns?"

Rory nodded.

"Very good. You and Bobbee must find a solution to this problem, but on one condition."

"Of course," said Bobbee. "And that condition is...?"

"That you keep our Bee World a secret,"

said Queen Bee.

Rory looked at the queen with understanding and nodded. Of course she wanted to keep the Bee World safe. If other humans knew about it, they would just destroy it.

With that, Queen Bee buzzed to the base of her hivequarters, and as she did so, a panel revealed itself which scanned her bee body with a red light. The red light then turned green, and the bottom of the hive extended out to reveal three human sized items: a pot of honey; a large piece of beeswax; and a tin of royal jelly.

"You must take this special toolkit with you. I know it will prove to be very useful for you both."

"What is—?" asked Rory, but Queen Bee had already started flying away.

"I wish you strength and the will to

succeed," she said as she buzzed away, "and as queen I must insist you keep me up to date please."

Chapter Four

The next morning, after Rory had stuffed his face with a stack of American pancakes that his dad had cooked for them all, Rory sat precariously on a wooden swing that hung from one of the rotten branches within the great oaks forest. Bobbee buzzed back and forth beside him, puffing and panting, trying to keep up.

"I hung this swing twenty-odd years ago for your mum to play on," Bobbee reminisced. "She would've been about your age."

"I can tell," said Rory as he inspected the severely frayed rope that looked like it was about to snap. He rocked back and forth on his heels with his feet firmly planted in the bone-dry soil. The fragile branch above him creaked with each to and fro as Rory wracked his brains as to what his first steps should be on his given mission.

Creak. Creak. Creak.

Rory halted suddenly.

"Thank goodness," said Bobbee, doubling over as he sank down to Rory's knee, looking like he was about to collapse with exhaustion.

"What about that magic formula we treated your mouldy cabbage plants with?" asked Rory. "That seemed to clean them up nicely."

"Ah, well, this is awkward," Bobbee confessed. "I used to tell you it was magic so that you'd be excited and help me. When really it actually wasn't very magic at all. I just needed to get some jobs done, and you needed entertaining whilst your mum and dad had to work. It was just a little homemade recipe that I came up with myself, sorry."

"It's fine," said Rory as he brushed off the disappointment. "I didn't really believe it was magic anyway."

"Yes, you did," said Bobbee playfully, nudging his arm.

Of course, Rory really had believed it. In fact, he had believed it so much so that when Grandad Bobbee had been too poorly to take him to Legoland for his birthday, Rory had made his own 'magic' formula out of peanut butter, marmite, and strawberry jam. He'd then spread it onto Grandad's toast so that he would be better again. It had made Grandad Bobbee feel even more queasy, truth be told, and sadly had not had any magic effects on his sickness. As Rory had believed in it so much though, Grandad Bobbee had pretended to be fine, and had got out of bed so that Rory could still have his special birthday trip.

"Alright, alright, I believed it. But I'm grown up now, so let's move on," said Rory dismissively. "What was so great about it anyway? What was the 'magic' ingredient?"

"Baking soda," said Bobbee. "I saw it in the bathroom cabinet one day and thought 'well if it can clean my teeth gently then maybe it can clean my plants'. I gave it a go and happens it did a pretty okay job."

"Baking soda? Interesting," said Rory curiously as he started to rock back and forth again, which gave Bobbee a 'here we go again' feeling. "So where could we get baking soda from out here? The shop isn't ever open," pondered Rory.

"Maybe there'll be something in Frank's pantry in the farmhouse," Bobbee said confidently. "His mother used to bake us some delightful Victoria sponge cakes when I was evacuated here in the war as a kid." Bobbee licked his lips as the memory set off his taste buds.

"We don't want one hundred year old baking soda though do we Grandad?" Rory shivered. "It could be riddled with bugs and would definitely not be effective at cleaning fungus."

Bobbee laughed at the insult disguised as science. "Very funny. I'll have you know that it wasn't quite that long ago, and I'm certain that Frank will have bought a new one since then!" he reassured Rory.

"Why don't you go and get it and I'll wait here," said Rory, who was propped up on the rope swing.

"How do you expect a teeny tiny bee to carry a container of baking soda that is probably at least twenty times the size of its head?" asked Bobbee.

"I've seen dung beetles carry poo twenty times the size of them on their backs," argued Rory playfully. "But fine, I'll go into the pantry and get the baking soda," he huffed. As he stood up from the rope swing, the creaking branch creaked for the last time and it crumbled away from its trunk and tumbled onto the ground with a thud, narrowly missing Rory's toes.

As Rory reached the farmhouse, he walked down the gravel side path and stood on his tiptoes on the edge of the step to peer through the glass in the top of the door. The pantry was right there in front of him, just as Bobbee had described. Inside, Rory saw a young girl sorting through tinned baked beans and tinned peaches on one of the many pantry shelves. Her blonde ponytail swished from left to right as she sorted. Farmer Frank's dog appeared from nowhere and began sniffing Rory's ankle. It tickled and made him jump out of his skin, causing him to slip off of the step and headbutt the glass.

Bang!

The dog ran off and the young girl turned and screamed when she saw Rory's face squished into the glass, knocking an entire shelf of tins to the floor in the process. Rory was dazed by the collision, but quickly opened the door and rushed to help.

"I'm so sorry, I didn't mean to scare you. The dog... I was just going to... I wanted to ask for... sorry, I'm Rory. I'm staying in one of the caravans," he stuttered.

"Yes, I know," she said. "You're the only family here."

"Good point," continued Rory awkwardly, as he knelt down on the cold terracotta tiled floor to collect several tins which had rolled underneath the pantry shelves.

"I'm Izzy, Frank's granddaughter. I'm staying for a few days," she said, reaching out a hand to shake his.

Rory didn't really communicate well at the best of times, and except for his mum and his little sister, he really didn't have too much to do with girls. The thought of holding hands with one made him feel a bit sheepish and weird, so instead, he raised his hand and gave a little tentative wave.

Izzy thought his behaviour was a little strange but dismissed it quickly. "How can I help you, anyway, Rory?" she asked.

Rory tried to think fast, and not unusually the first thing that came into his mind was food. He always ate when he was panicked.

"Pancakes," he blurted out.

"I'm afraid we don't have pancakes, just a few tins of beans and peaches. Basic stuff," she said.

Rory put his brain back in gear and remembered what he was there for. "Sorry, I mean we need baking soda. Mum is making pancakes for lunch," he stumbled. "Might you have some we can borrow? I'll bring it back."

"Sounds delicious," she said. "Don't you usually eat pancakes for breakfast though?"

"Yes, we had them this morning," said Rory, not thinking before he spoke.

"And you're having them for lunch too?" asked Izzy.

Rory began to flap. "Breakfast, lunch and dinner in our house. Mum is pretty skilled at savoury and sweet ones," Rory rambled.

Izzy turned to the shelf, hunting high and low. "Frank is pretty much a beans-on-toast-

and-a-tin-of-peaches-with-cream-if-you're-lucky kind of Grandad. But not for breakfast. Breakfast is toast. Plain with butter. Every day." She sifted through all the containers and pulled out a small pot. "Seems we have baking powder, but not baking soda. Is that the same thing?"

"I'll take it and give it a go. Thank you so much," said Rory in a rush, eager to escape.

"You're welcome," said Izzy. She watched as he disappeared as fast as he could walk and called out to him. "Maybe I'll see you later? After your pancakes?"

Rory was too focused on his mission to hear her.

Chapter Five

Bobbee was resting on the grounded branch, contemplating the enormity of the task ahead, when Rory bounded over to him like a giddy puppy, waving the 'magic' ingredient. He ground to a halt before he tripped.

"She only had baking powder. I'm not sure if that's the same thing?" he puffed.

"You've met Izzy then? Isn't she a sweetie?" Bobbee smiled.

Rory glossed over the comment and looked down at his watch. "Grandad, how are we going to get rid of the fungus? What's our plan?"

"Right-o," said Bobbee as he clapped his bee hands together eagerly. "We'll need to get a damp sponge first. Then we'll sprinkle on the powder and apply some elbow grease."

"There's a sponge beside the kitchen sink in the caravan, but I'm not sure I've seen any elbow grease. Might Izzy have that in the pantry too?" asked Rory, curiously.

Bobbee laughed. "It's just a turn of phrase kid. It means we'll give it a good old scrub."

"Why didn't you just say that then?" said Rory rolling his eyes. He knew Grandad Bobbee would have hours of fun teasing him, but Rory didn't mind – it wasn't to upset or offend him. It was just their little joke that they shared.

Bobbee sat comfortably on Rory's head, draped in a sumptuous jacket that he had fashioned out of his silky red hair. He directed Rory to stand on the precarious fallen branch so that he could reach a knot in the rotten tree trunk with his right foot, but Rory delayed, thinking.

"Mum was asking loads of questions about why I needed the sponge. I just told her that it was part of my school project and that I would be spending a lot of time in the forest working hard on it," he said. "That won't have upset the queen, will it?"

"No, of course not. That was good thinking kid," said Bobbee. "We both know what a worrier she can be."

The tree knot was sunken in just enough

to allow the toe of Rory's trainers to rest there. He felt for a piece of jagged bark to grip with his hands, and reached for it, but it came away with a *crack*, wobbling him not only physically but mentally too. Rory was the epitome of existing within one's comfort zone. If it wasn't Lego or his laptop then he was on edge.

"Don't panic, don't panic," said Bobbee, trying to reassure him. "Just take a breath, look for another grip and try again."

Rory refocused and took a big deep breath. His heart pounded in his chest.

Ba-boom. Ba-Boom. Ba-Boom.

He looked up and around, reaching for another piece of bark to grip hold of. Slowly, he let the bark take his weight, awaiting the crack and inevitable fall. To his relief, he pulled and pulled and moved his trailing foot from the fallen log into the tree knot to meet the other, and proudly sat up on a sturdy looking branch.

"Well done," praised Bobbee. "Now, take the baking powder and sprinkle it onto a leaf just like you'd do with icing sugar on a Victoria sponge cake. Then make it into a paste by rubbing it in gently with the damp sponge."

Rory understood the instructions and took the baking powder from his back pocket and shook a little onto a leaf, working it into a sticky paste with the sponge. Nothing happened.

"Did we get the pretend magic formula wrong?" he asked Grandad.

"Nope, it's the very same. Maybe if you rub some more into the same spot?"

Rory rubbed in some more of the paste and noted that the leaf became less dull looking this time. He gently wiped the leaf and it began to look a sort of green again.

"It's working!" exclaimed Rory excitedly.

"How marvellous," said Bobbee. "Then keep going. We've no time to delay." Rory scrubbed another one quickly and another and another and another and another.

"This is amazing. All we have to do now is clean the entire forest. Then the visitors will return again and Farmer Frank will have his livelihood back. He'll be so pleased," Rory celebrated.

But as quickly as the leaves had turned bright green again, they started to turn a dull mucky pond colour.

"Uh oh," worried Rory, as they continued to change colour.

The leaves turned orange, then yellow, then finally black. Pitch black. To Rory's horror, they then separated themselves from the tree and fell to the ground like stones, turning to dust on the forest floor.

"No, no, no, no, no! What did I do wrong?" Rory said in shock as he looked down at the ground, devastated.

"You didn't do anything wrong," said Bobbee, trying to console him. "I don't think we are dealing with any ordinary kind of fungus here. We are going to need a much bigger idea to beat it."

As Rory lifted his eye gaze from the ground, a gleaming black car turned into the campsite entrance, catching both Rory and Bobbee's attention.

"Who is that?" asked Bobbee.

"I don't know, but it looks like an official kind of car," said Rory as the shiny black paintwork kept coming and coming and coming. It was the length of a bus, and only just fit onto the dusty driveway in front of the farmhouse.

"That is no ordinary car," said Bobbee. "It's a limousine."

"Wow!" said Rory. "It must belong to someone very important."

"Quick, let's get down and take a look," said Bobbee.

Rory and Bobbee watched from the ground as the driver of the limousine opened his door and stepped onto the dusty gravel of the driveway. It crunched underfoot and puffed dust up into the air, which made his shiny black shoes and trousers dirty. He walked purposefully several paces beside the sparkling car and opened the rear door on the drivers' side. Out stepped a mysterious black brogue-style shoe that glowed in the sunlight like a beacon; not a pretty, twinkling star-at-night type beacon, but a menacing torchlight-in-the-dead-of-night type. The black shiny brogue belonged to an expensive black suit called Mr Zemmer. He had a pristine white collar with a precisely knotted tie. His short wet-looking black hair had a very precise parting.

The driver opened up the boot of the limousine and handed Mr Zemmer a black leather briefcase from inside. The businessman tucked it under his arm and climbed the concrete step to Farmer Frank's door. He knocked slowly and loudly three times, which made the walls of the house rumble and the paint peel.

Bobbee shivered from his bee sting to his bee nose as he watched the front door open and Farmer Frank welcome him in.

"Are you okay, Grandad?" asked Rory.

"My bee sting is vibrating which tells me that there is something verrry fishy going on here."

The driver casually leant against the

vehicle with his back to the open boot. He took out his mobile phone from his pocket and started to scroll through it.

"Are you thinking what I'm thinking?" asked Rory.

"Well, I was hoping you might be wondering what's for tea, but I have this funny feeling that you want to climb into that boot and follow the suited-man to find out who he is," squeaked Bobbee.

"You always were good at reading my mind. Let's go," said Rory determinedly, as he ran off at super speed.

"Wait, let me get this straight," whispered Bobbee as he buzzed behind him, praying that he could discourage Rory. "You want to climb into the boot of that limousine to go goodness knows where?"

"Yes, I do. But don't worry, we'll be in goodness knows where together. We have to get to the bottom of this," said Rory.

The doorknob to Farmer Frank's front door began to turn.

"Hold on Grandad!" Rory warned, and Bobbee held on tightly to Rory's red hair as if he was riding a wild and wayward horse.

"Woah!" Bobbee yelled.

"We have to make it into that boot before he—"

Mr Zemmer appeared from behind Farmer Frank's door.

"I'll give it some thought, Mr Zemmer," said Farmer Frank reluctantly, as he ushered the businessman out.

"Please do," said Mr Zemmer. "Imagine the lives of the families that will be changed by having such a wonderful organic vegetable farm right here at Great Oaks." He handed Frank a wodge of paper which read 'contract of sale' on the front. "Just take a look at what we are offering. It is a handsome sum that will afford you a charming beachfront bungalow somewhere, perfect for your retirement."

Rory put his head down and ran purposefully, swinging his arms like there was no tomorrow. Bobbee bounced around as they bounded toward Farmer Frank's front door, and just as Mr Zemmer began to turn his head and face in their direction, Rory leapt headfirst into a bush to hide.

There was a moment of stillness.

"Are you okay, Grandad?" Rory asked again as he pushed the leaves from in front of his face aside, allowing him to see Farmer Frank close the door behind Mr Zemmer.

"Yes, I think so," Bobbee said as he checked himself over.

The businessman took the few steps back towards the limousine.

"Now he is going to hand the briefcase to the driver, who will return it to the boot. We need to be inside there before it shuts," commanded Rory.

"So, when he puts his hand out, we need to run around the back of the limousine and jump into the boot before the case goes inside?" asked Bobbee.

"Exactly," confirmed Rory. The driver put out his hand to take the briefcase. "Move, move, move," barked Rory like he was a sergeant major.

Rory crouched down and stealthily navigated his way around the limousine, leaping into the boot and laying down without making a sound. The driver placed the briefcase down inside without paying any due care and attention to the contents of the boot, and he shut the lid. Rory and Bobbee lay in complete darkness.

"I hate the dark, Grandad," said Rory, realising what he had just done.

"I know you do kid, but we have a mission to complete and there is no way that Mr Zemmer's 'organic vegetable farm' is real. We just need to prove it."

"Mum is going to be so upset when she realises that I'm missing, isn't she?" said Rory.

"She won't find out. She'll think that you're still working on your school project in the forest. We'll be home by dinnertime," said Bobbee hopefully.

Chapter Six

Rory and Bobbee were completely oblivious to their location as they lay in the pitch black of the limousine boot, waiting for the car to reach its destination.

"I think we're here," said Bobbee, sensing that they had stopped moving.

"Where's here? That's what I want to know," said Rory.

They both flinched as they heard the limousine doors opening and slamming shut.

"They're getting out," whispered Bobbee.

"You think?" whispered Rory sarcastically, before a streak of blinding daylight hit him square in the eyes as the driver opened the boot and reached in to pick up the briefcase. Then he slammed it shut again.

"We are going to need a hairpin to pick that lock," declared Rory, feeling more confident.

"No, we won't," said Bobbee.

"Yes, we will. I've seen it on TV a million times," he said.

Bobbee pulled out a torch from his bee backpack, buzzed towards the boot lock, and engaged his stinger.

"What are you doing?" asked Rory.

"Just something that I learned in bee school," he said, as he wiggled his stinger around in the lock in a figure of eight motion. The boot lid popped, pinging open. "I've still got it," said Bobbee, pleased with himself as he stood on the boot ledge holding out his

74

bee hand to high-five Rory.

Rory reached out a finger pad for the celebration. "Amazing Grandad. Let's go!" cheered Rory.

Bobbee used Rory's finger to vault up and onto the back of his hand. Rory leapt out of the boot. As he did, he got his foot caught on a camel-coloured coat that Mr Zemmer had left behind.

"So this is what freedom feels like," said Rory as he looked up. And up. And then up some more. He craned his neck at the massive glass office building in front of him, adorned with the title 'Zemmer Enterprises' at the very top. The entire building was made out of huge panels of pristine and sparkling glass that reached the sky. A window cleaner was twirling his squeegee as he abseiled from a mechanical platform.

"Wow. I bet he feels like spiderman," Rory

commented, shifting his gaze to look inside the building.

Mr Zemmer and his driver were making their way towards the electronic security gate within the lobby of the building. Mr Zemmer pulled out his pass and swiped it over the scanner, but the gate wouldn't open. He sighed and swiped again. Again, the gates refused to open.

"Oh for goodness' sake, when are we going to get these gates fixed?" he exclaimed scornfully, staring straight at the receptionist.

"Sorry Mr Zemmer. I'll let you through," she said nervously. Suddenly both sides of the gate retracted, and the receptionist waved Mr Zemmer and his driver through.

Rory looked at Bobbee, and Bobbee looked at Rory.

"How are we going to get through

security?" asked Bobbee.

"Right now I have no clue," said Rory, just as the receptionist on duty changed shift and another receptionist took her place. Rory thought quickly.

"Pass me that coat, Grandad," said Rory. "I have an idea."

Bobbee buzzed back into the open boot of the limousine and heaved the long camel coloured coat out with his tiny bee body.

"Let's hope it fits," said Rory, as he draped it around his shoulders.

Bobbee turned up the collar on the coat to create a distraction from the fact that the coat dragged along the floor. Rory put his hands in the pockets and found a beanie hat. He placed it over his head before walking towards the gate. Bobbee hid in the sort of tunnel that had formed between the upturned collar of the coat and Rory's neck. As he walked, slowly, Rory marvelled at the marble flooring and huge palm trees, and wondered quite how they had got something quite so massive inside. His eyes glazed over as he thought hard about it. Had they used a crane and dropped it in through the ceiling? Or perhaps it had been grown from a little tiny seed in the huge pot it now resided in? Rory was often branded 'easily distracted' by his teachers, but the truth of it was that he had a very curious mind. He needed to know just how everything worked and why it worked. It's how he was able to be quite so inventive because he was always concerned about making things work better or more easily. Bobbee clicked his bee fingers to get Rory's attention,

"This is no time to fall asleep. This is just getting good," said Bobbee enthusiastically.

Rory snapped out of his dream state and

his vision crispened. "I'm not asleep, I'm getting myself into character before we head on in."

"Head on in to where though?" asked Bobbee.

Rory tapped his chin, deep in thought, as a cleaner passed through the lobby dragging a mop and bucket behind him on the marble floor. They watched as he unlocked a door in the far corner underneath the curved marble staircase. "We'll head straight into that cupboard and then we'll come up with a next step there."

Rory tried to look inconspicuous and faced away from the reception desk as he arrived at the security gates. He reached into his pocket and lifted out his bus pass and hovered it over the scanner. It failed to open. Suddenly, Rory's physical posture changed. He stood taller and lifted his shoulders back and growled.

"Oh for goodness' sake, when are we going to get these gates fixed?" he bellowed, mimicking Mr Zemmer's voice.

"I'm so sorry Mr Zemmer, I'll buzz you through," the receptionist responded apologetically as the gates retracted.

Rory marched through like a man on a mission, and once he was past the reception, he scurried with a body full of adrenaline and bounded into the cleaning cupboard. With his back to the wall, he slid down and hugged his knees into his chest to make himself as small as he could. Bobbee buzzed up onto Rory's knees, grinning from ear to ear.

"I'm impressed kid. That was brilliant."

"That was the most scary but fun thing I've ever done," giggled Rory.

"It really was," said Bobbee. "But as much as I'd love to laugh right now, we must focus our attention on locating Mr Zemmer. We know that he went up the stairs, but we need to find out where they lead and what he is hiding."

"Do we *really*?" asked Rory, with a tilt of his head.

"Come on kid, you're good at this now," said Bobbee, trying to fill him with some confidence.

Rory took a breath and then jumped to his feet, grabbing the cleaner's overalls from behind the cupboard door and placing Mr Zemmer's coat there instead. Bobbee took up residence in the crook of Rory's neck, hiding himself in his grandson's hair. They peered around the door of the cupboard to check that the coast was clear. The receptionist tapped away at her keyboard which echoed in the empty marble lobby. Rory made a run for the stairs. He tried to emulate the sound of the keyboard by tip tapping with his feet across the marble floor.

"Left or right?" said Bobbee as they reached the top of the stairs.

Rory glanced right and then left along the clinically white corridor. There were doors on both sides, approximately five metres apart from each other, and each of them had a small rectangular glass panel above the door handle. Heading right, Rory crouched down below one of the panels and looked in through the keyhole.

"It's empty," he whispered to Bobbee.

"Okay, next," Bobbee responded.

Rory stayed crouched down and shuffled on all fours like a gorilla to the next door.

Again, he peered through the glass. There, sat opposite his driver, was Mr Zemmer. Rory pointed at the door to confirm to Bobbee that they had the correct room this time. Bobbee buzzed away from Rory's blanket of hair to sit on the edge of the keyhole and look through.

"Can you hear what they're saying?" whispered Rory.

"No, they're too far away. I think we need to use this," he said, as he reached into his bee backpack and rifled around. Then he pulled out a tiny gadget that was as small as a pin head.

"What is that?" asked Rory

"It's a listening device," said Bobbee. "I'll buzz in and plant it beside the light switch and we'll be able to make some sense of the conversation." Before Rory could stop him, Bobbee buzzed through the keyhole and fixed the gadget to the light switch, quickly returning to Rory. Then he reached into his bee backpack again and pulled out a radio device. They listened intently through headphones.

"Is everything ready for the investor meeting?" asked Mr Zemmer.

"Yes sir. The presentation is all set up in the conference room already," said the driver.

"How many are we expecting?" asked Mr Zemmer.

"Around the one hundred and twenty mark I believe."

"One hundred and twenty?" Rory gasped. "That's a lot of people wanting to buy Farmer Frank's land."

"If we can get even half the investors on board we will be the biggest luxury resort in the region," said Mr Zemmer as he rubbed his hands together gleefully.

"Wait, what?" said Rory, doing a double take, "They're not turning the site into organic farmland at all?"

"I knew that there was something unsettling about this guy," said Bobbee. "A luxury resort, eh?"

"That's dreadful. What about the trees? The wildlife? The farmers' livelihoods? It's all going to be ruined," said Rory furiously.

"Not on our watch it isn't, don't you worry," said Bobbee passionately.

A cleaner approached with a mop and bucket, catching the duo by surprise. Rory and Bobbee quickly put their heads down, but the cleaner passed by without even a second glance. Suddenly, Rory's nose started to tingle. There was a strange scent lingering in the air.

"Can you smell that, Grandad? It smells

terribly familiar," said Rory curiously.

"Can't say that I do," said Bobbee.

"I must be imagining it," said Rory, trying to be dismissive, but his nose tingled again. "I can smell it again, Grandad. It smells just like the forest," he said, with his nose in the air and a disgusted look on his face. He noticed a tiny drip of liquid on the floor and knelt down, putting his nose right to it. "That's why it smells like the forest, Grandad. It's the fungus I can smell!"

"Are you sure?" asked Bobbee.

"Sure I'm sure. We need to retrace the steps of that cleaner and find out exactly what is going on here," said Rory, as he looked down the corridor to see a trail of intermittent drips. They followed them down the light and bright corridor. The further they went, the darker their surroundings became, until only the dim light of the odd spotlight in the ceiling lit their way. They walked and walked and walked, making sure to keep looking over their shoulders to check that they weren't being followed. When they eventually reached the end of the corridor, they discovered a door. A single white door. It had no handle. It had no security keypad. It had no glass panel. It had no keyhole.

"There's no way in," said Bobbee.

"Of course there is," said Rory positively, which raised an eyebrow from Bobbee. "We just don't know how to get in yet. Come on, think, Rory, think."

After lots of thinking, the door suddenly opened and a lady wearing a white lab coat came out. Rory, with Bobbee on his shoulder, turned away and looked down, as if he was cleaning the floor. But his eyes glanced back to the crack in the door. A blindingly bright light shone in his face, but just as it did, it was gone, and the door closed again. The lady in the lab coat kept walking.

"Spiderman, Grandad," said Rory through gritted teeth.

"What's spiderman got to do with anything?" asked Bobbee.

"The window cleaner," said Rory. "When the door opened, sunlight shone straight into my face. That means that there is a window inside there, and to be able to look through it and see what exactly is going on here, we are going to need to borrow that window cleaner's platform."

"But you're afraid of heights." said Bobbee.

"The need to know what is in that room is somehow making me less afraid," Rory said bravely.

Chapter Seven

Rory and Bobbee left the building through the nearest fire exit, skirting around its long glassy exterior in search of the window cleaner's platform. Rory rushed ahead.

"This way," he said.

Bobbee followed as Rory stepped onto the platform, which wobbled underfoot. Rory's anxiety skyrocketed. He hated heights more than anything. Bobbee landed on the control pad in the corner, which was made up of a joystick and several buttons, including a big round red one.

"I wonder what the red one does?" asked Bobbee.

"Being risk-averse and feeling quite sick, I'm going to say let's not find out. Without a manual of how this thing works, we are going to have to start pressing some buttons quickly," said Rory, who was trying to spread his weight evenly across the platform by stretching both legs out to make a wide base – something he'd learnt in gym at school.

Bobbee charged at the control pad, all gung-ho.

"Wait!" shouted Rory. "Can't you just buzz up there and see if you can see the window?"

"I wish that it was that straight forward but no, it would be far too windy up there. I'd just get knocked out of the sky and splatted onto the nearest skyscraper," explained Bobbee.

"I'm fairly sure that bees can fly really

high, Grandad," said Rory.

"Alright, alright, you've got me. I'm a bee who was once a human who was scared of heights. I'd really rather have this platform than have to take off up there where there aren't any handrails."

"Fine," said Rory as he simultaneously squeezed his eyelids shut in fear then opened them in excitement as he put his right hand on the joystick and pushed it forwards. But nothing happened. Which was kind of a relief, but also frustrating, all mixed into one crazy emotion.

"Try one of the black buttons," said Bobbee.

Rory closed his eyes shut and asked himself what a secret agent would do. Then he whacked the red button, which sent them skywards.

"Wooooooooah!" exclaimed Rory as the

platform scaled the side of the building. He held on to the metal frame with all his might. "I think I'm going to throw up."

"Me too! Make it stop. Please make it stop," Bobbee begged.

Rory opened his eyes and whacked the red button again with an open hand. The platform stopped. All was still. Until out of the blue, Bobbee's visor phone began to ring. He tilted the visor down over his eyes which made him look like a kind of fighter pilot ready to do battle. Without realising that she could already be seen, Queen Bee pouted and preened herself. Bobbee smiled to himself, then answered the call with a serious face. "Yes, Your Majesty?"

"How is one getting on, Bobbee?" she asked with her silky royal tone.

"One is doing very well," said Bobbee as he looked at Rory, who was laughing at his pretend posh accent.

"And the mission? Are we expected to be through to completion shortly?" she asked hopefully.

Bobbee had no idea how to answer, but knew that if he didn't get her off the call soon, they stood a high chance of falling off a window cleaner's platform onto the pavement below.

"Young Rory has a plan Your Majesty and is working towards that plan with good humour and grace," he said, forming any words he could think of that sounded like he had it covered.

"Good humour and grace?" said Queen Bee spiritedly, "I expect nothing short of tenacity and excellence, you hear?" With that the line went dead.

Bobbee pulled his visor back up.

"Is one okay?" said Rory, mimicking

Bobbee's ridiculous accent.

"Shall we just get on with it?" said Bobbee with a sigh. "We now know that the red button is 'on'. Now, how do we get to the window that you *thought* you saw?"

"I didn't 'think' I saw a window, Grandad. I definitely did see a window. The sun was blasting through it. So given the sun rises in the east and sets in the west, and we are currently facing north, and it's 2pm, we know that the window must be on this side of the building."

"Well thank goodness for that," said Bobbee, reassured that he didn't have to scale any other parts of the building. "Now we just have to find the window."

"That can't be too difficult. We were on the second floor when we followed the drip trail, and by my reckoning we are now on the third. Let's drop the joystick down slowly and see what happens."

Bobbee buzzed over to the joystick and yanked it downwards, which made the platform descend slowly to the second floor.

"Okay stop."

Bobbee brought the joystick back to the middle of the control pad.

"Now use the black button on the left to travel westwards."

Bobbee hit the black button to the left of the joystick and the platform moved left. They could see offices. Then a gym. And then a cafeteria.

"Okay, nothing that way. Let's try east," Rory directed as Bobbee pushed the joystick to the right, which sent the platform to the right.

They went back past the cafeteria. The gym. The offices. To a conference room with a big screen and a picture titled 'Zemmer

Luxury Resort & Spa'.

"Keep going, keep going, keep..." said Rory, until finally they made it to the far-right corner of the building. "Where is the window then?" said Rory, now frustrated.

"You must've imagined it," said Bobbee.

Rory kept nudging the platform left and right and up and down, until a light reflected on the right of his face. He looked right to see a small mirror attached to a tree that was reflecting the sun back towards the building.

"They're channelling the sunlight. So there must be a really small window in the shade here somewhere," he said as he peered around the corner of the building.

His keen eyes caught sight of a tiny window the size of a jam jar. He looked through it and it confirmed their worst fears. A pristine white room with several staff members tottering around in white lab coats... and several large vats of bubbling pink liquid.

"It seems that Mr Zemmer is cooking up the fungus that is destroying Great Oaks. He's poisoning everything so that nobody wants to visit anymore, forcing Farmer Frank and his peers to sell to make way for Zemmer's beloved resort."

Bobbee used his binoculars to get a clearer view, and they saw what looked like a conveyor belt with several spouts hanging above it, popping out spherical pink objects.

"What on Earth are those?" said Bobbee.

"He's making paintballs! And he's using Travis to do his dirty work for him by aiming at – and missing – his friends in the forest. Very devious indeed. We have to stop him Grandad. Do you have any images of the forest?" asked Rory.

"All stored on the memory card," said Bobbee as he tapped his bee backpack.

"Perfect, then I will leave this one to you Grandad," said Rory with a wink.

Dozens of wealthy looking investors began to filter into the Zemmer Enterprises conference room excitedly. Bobbee buzzed over their heads towards the front of the room in a zig zag fashion, to avoid the wafting hands of the delegates as they tried to swipe him out of the air space. Mr Zemmer was standing front and centre, his hands clenched, ready to address his audience. Bobbee gave him a wide berth, trying to locate and circle in on the laptop and the inserted memory card. Behind him was a screen with a holding-slide.

Bobbee made it to the laptop, which was plugged into a projector, and perched on it next to the inserted memory card. He couldn't help but feel a little debilitated: he was heaving with all of his might to try and remove the card but his little bee body couldn't budge it. Mr Zemmer cleared his throat, ready to begin. Bobbee scrunched up his face with determination and kept on trying.

"Welcome everyone, to what is to be a most fortuitous day for you all. I know that I need no introduction, but I have an exciting proposition to introduce you to. Imagine for a moment, if you will, a sprawling resort of gargantuan proportions, boasting several outdoor tennis courts, a championship golf course, a spa, a formula one racetrack, sumptuous suites and two Michelin star restaurants. Imagine waking up in the morning after a dreamy night's sleep and opening your curtains to these views."

Bobbee heaved and heaved and heaved, now in a flat panic, just as Mr Zemmer reached for his clicker to move to the next slide. The memory card began to move and as it pinged out of the laptop it launched Bobbee backwards with it and he splatted against the wall. With no time to spare, he picked himself up and charged towards the laptop. Pulling out a gold memory card from his bee backpack he pushed it into the slot just in the nick of time. Mr Zemmer looked into the audience with complete arrogance written across his face, but instead of the audience 'ooh-ing' and 'ahh-ing', they gasped in absolute horror at the image before them. Mr Zemmer turned to his presentation and was greeted by an image of the ugly, rotting devastation that was Great Oaks Forest.

"I have no idea how that got there," he fussed. "How about I show you the kitchen gardens of our Michelin star restaurant?"

Mr Zemmer quickly tried to click through to the next slide, but the next slide was of one of the neighbouring farms and its vegetables, all of which had been completely devastated by the fungus.

"Oh goodness," he said, "There has to be some sort of mistake. One moment." He frantically clicked through to the next slide.

A film started playing, recorded by Bobbee, showing the Zemmer Enterprises building and the fungus production in the on-site laboratory. One by one, the disgusted investors filed out of the conference room.

Chapter Eight

Outside of the Zemmer Enterprises building, Rory and Bobbee were reunited.

"Great work Grandad," said Rory, raising his hand for a high-five.

Bobbee flew into Rory's finger pad with his hand raised. Just as he did, Mr Zemmer left through the front of the building and his driver opened the passenger door to the limousine. Rory and Bobbee could just about make out what was being said.

"Mr Zemmer?" called a nasal female voice.

Mr Zemmer turned to see a short woman in a sharp suit with slicked-back blonde hair tied neatly into a ponytail. "I am willing to fully invest in this resort, but on one condition."

"Which is?" said Mr Zemmer.

"The fungus is part of the deal," she said.

Mr Zemmer reached out a hand and she shook it firmly.

"What are we going to do now?" asked Rory, as he sank himself to the pavement and pulled his knees in towards his chest. "We're never going to save the forest." He felt so glum that he reached into his toolkit and pulled out the jar of honey. He unscrewed the lid.

Bobbee looked at him firmly. "I wouldn't do that if I were you."

"What?" said Rory. "When I'm worried, I eat."

Rory dipped his fingers into it and was

about to put them into his mouth when Bobbee buzzed like a dart straight onto the end of Rory's nose. He eyeballed Rory, forcing him to go cross-eyed.

"That is no ordinary honey remember," said Bobbee firmly.

"Huh?" said Rory, with his mouth gaping open.

"It has special healing properties, and therefore it is imperative that you..." Bobbee tapped Rory on the nose with his stinger. "Do. Not. Waste. A. Single. Drop."

"Owww!" cried Rory, waving his two fingers in circles in the air as he tried to keep the honey from falling. "What do I do with it if it isn't for eating?" asked Rory.

"Well, that is up to you," said Bobbee. "But it better be good. Queen Bee is expecting something quite marvellous from you."

Rory tried to screw the lid back onto the

honey but couldn't whilst flapping his fingers about, so without thinking he shoved his fingers into his mouth and licked off the honey, and then screwed the lid back on. Bobbee looked at him in horror.

"Whoops, sorry Grandad," said Rory embarrassed.

"Time to make that old farmer an offer that he can't refuse this time," said Mr Zemmer to his driver, as he parted company with the investor. The driver opened the limousine passenger door. "The car will take too long. Have the chopper ready at the helipad for me immediately."

"Yes sir," said the driver, as he reached into his pocket for his phone. He dialled a number, then held it to his ear. "Have a chopper ready on the helipad immediately, Captain. Mr Zemmer wants to make an urgent visit to Great Oaks."

"That's our ride home," said Bobbee. "But where is the helipaaaaaaad?"

Rory had hit the red button and the platform was soaring up towards the roof of the building, leaving both of them clinging on for dear life.

Chuff chuff chuff chuff chuff chuff

As they reached the very top of the Zemmer Enterprises building, all they could hear was a helicopter's rotors spinning fiercely. Rory managed to scurry across the helipad, holding onto Bobbee all the way so he didn't get blown away. Just as Rory climbed inside the luggage hold and closed the door, the helicopter started to lift from the helipad, kicking up a cyclone of dust.

"We really need to stop travelling like this," said Rory, who had a suitcase leaning against his face. The helicopter bounced around the skies, throwing them both this way and that. "Now I know why they call this a chopper, Grandad."

"Yes, it is a bit choppy, isn't it?" said Bobbee, as they both kept bumping their heads on the shelf above them.

"Please tell me this will all be over soon?" begged Rory.

"They're just clouds, Rory," said Bobbee softly. "We are just bumping through them. Imagine you're on the back of a giant bird soaring through the sky. Every time there is a cloud it bumps up and over it, through to clearer air."

Rory squeezed his eyes shut to imagine this. A few silent moments passed before...

"Clouds! That's it, Grandad!" yelled Rory

excitedly as his eyes pinged wide open.

"That's what?" asked Bobbee.

"When clouds get heavy with too much moisture, that's when we get rain. We learnt it in school."

"Very impressive. But what's rain got to do with anything?"

"Well, we are above the clouds right now, aren't we? So if I trickle some of this special healing honey into the clouds, maybe it will rain honey all over the great oak trees and make them great again."

"That could work," said Bobbee.

"What do you mean it *could* work? It *has* to work, otherwise Farmer Frank will sell his land to Mr Zemmer and all the forest and the nature within it will die."

Rory carefully nudged opened the window of the luggage hold and looked out onto the grey cloudy sky as the wind blew right into his face, making his skin ripple. He twisted the lid off the honey jar, pausing as he watched for something that looked familiar beneath them. All of a sudden, he saw a black and white ant-sized creature beneath them, doing circles around a toy-sized car.

"That's Farmer Frank's dog down there, Grandad," he said triumphantly. "Right there. See?"

Bobbee peered over the window ledge, very keen to not get sucked out and swept away in the slipstream. "Yes I see! That's brilliant, Rory. Let's make Great Oaks great again," he declared, as Rory carefully started to pour the honey.

The thick, oozy liquid drizzled out of the window and into the clouds below as they flew overhead. Just as the last of the honey was poured, the helicopter began its descent into Great Oaks.

The helicopter landed in the pink fungus covered field opposite Farmer Frank's house. Rory and Bobbee watched from the luggage hold as the rotors raced around and around and kicked up dust everywhere. Mr Zemmer appeared from the helicopter cockpit and held his briefcase tightly to his chest as he scurried across the field and onto Farmer Frank's drive, before knocking on his door loudly three times.

As the coast was now clear, the duo jumped out from the luggage hold and onto the field.

"Am I pleased to see you," said Rory as he knelt down and kissed the dry ground. "Now all we need is some rain," he said, as he got up and looked into the dark sky.

"It does look a bit grim, doesn't it?" said Bobbee.

"The forest, or the sky?" asked Rory.

"Everything, I'm afraid," said Bobbee, as he parked his bee bottom on a pebble.

He looked down at the dusty soil and felt sadness rising inside him, but within seconds, a massive drop of rain pelted him on the back of the head. Then another came. And another. Bobbee's frown turned upside down. He looked up at Rory who was sat opposite him on a large rock, looking around at the forest. Why did it still look so dark and miserable.

"I don't understand, Grandad. What did I do wrong?" asked Rory, putting his head in his hands.

"I don't know," said Bobbee, who also put his head in his hands.

Time stood still as they both wondered if the honey really was magic after all. Then, out of nowhere, a single bluebell burst up through the forest floor at hyper speed right beneath where Bobbee was sitting, lifting him up towards Rory's fallen face like a beacon of hope. Bobbee peered through his fingers, dazzled by the bright and beautiful flower beneath him. As he removed his hand excitedly, he could see a glow rising from the forest floor.

"Rory! It worked! It worked!" cried Bobbee as he buzzed towards Rory's head with glee.

Rory slowly removed his hands from his face and saw the joyful sight before him. A golden ball of light swept through the forest, high and low before them like a sort of magic carpet rippling and spreading its power. First a blanket of bluebells popped up across the forest floor. Then the black bark on the trees peeled away, revealing healthy brown bark beneath. The canopies of the trees sprouted luscious, green leaves, their branches heaving with acorns. Jays flew through the trees and mice ran across the branches. Rory and Bobbee stood and watched in awe, their mouths gaping open.

"Now everyone will come back! Farmer Frank won't have to sell!" exclaimed Rory, delighted.

Slam!

His joy was halted abruptly as Farmer Frank's front door slammed behind a very smug looking Mr Zemmer. He held on tightly to the contract of sale as he ran back toward the waiting helicopter. The sight awakened the twosome from their happy place and Rory looked on with total dread.

"What on Earth are we going to do now?"

"I have absolutely no clue. But I know you will think of *something*," said Bobbee.

Chapter Nine

The next morning, Rory sat engrossed at his laptop in his bedroom, searching for answers and possible ways they could save the forest from destruction. Bobbee was playing basketball with a screwed-up piece of paper and Rory's water glass. He missed the glass and hit Rory in the face.

"Oops, sorry," said Bobbee.

"Please can you help me work out how to protect Great Oaks before that scoundrel Mr Zemmer gets his way and bulldozes it down so he can afford a fleet of new helicopters or whatever?" pleaded Rory.

"Of course, what can I do?" Bobbee asked eagerly.

"What do you know about preservation?" queried Rory.

"I used to preserve lemons from our lemon tree. You need a lot of salt," said Bobbee matter-of-factly.

"Not preserving lemons, Grandad. I mean preservation orders for trees. If we can prove that they are big enough, or old enough, then we might be able to get someone official to rip up that contract of sale because Mr Zemmer would be acting against the law."

"Wow, you really are clever, kid. How on Earth did you come up with that?" asked Bobbee, amazed.

"I just did an internet search, Grandad. I'll

teach you how one day," teased Rory.

"Rory! What drink would you like to take on the picnic today?" enquired Mum as she appeared at his bedroom door. "We have red squash or orange?"

"I can't come on a picnic, I'm afraid. I have far too much work to do in the forest," said Rory convincingly.

"You've been working so hard ever since you arrived. It will do you good to have a rest," Mum said hopefully.

"Before we came you said it would do me good to get into nature, and I think it *is* doing me good," said Rory. "My school project is fun, and I'm actually starting to like it here."

"I know, darling, but we miss you," Mum frowned.

"I will definitely spend tomorrow with you all," promised Rory.

"Deal," agreed Mum as she left his

bedroom. She then turned back briefly. "I'm really proud of you," she said with a smile.

"Thanks Mum," blushed Rory as she walked away. Bobbee pushed the door closed.

"So, how do you ask a tree its age?" asked Rory.

"Well, there is a folklore that says that you can age a tree by giving it a hug," Bobbee offered.

Rory raised both eyebrows.

"It's true. If you stretch out both of your arms around the girth of a tree trunk, a whole arm span is representative of one hundred years of age. So if you can get your arm span around a tree three times, then it is said to be three hundred years old," Bobbee explained.

"Wow that's almost as old as you!" laughed Rory.

Bobbee laughed and smirked

simultaneously.

"Right then. These trees won't hug themselves," said Rory.

Rory stood at the foot of a majestic oak tree and reached out his arms wide. Bobbee looked on.

"Stretch as far as you can because the folklore is really for an adults arm span."

"What are you doing?" Izzy asked, appearing stealthily by Rory's side.

Rory pulled his arms back down. "Nothing," he said dismissively. "I was just err... um... having a bit of a stretch before I go for a long run. Yes, that's exactly what I was doing."

"You hate long distance running," Bobbee laughed. Rory immediately tried to swat him into silence.

"Shouldn't you be stretching your legs instead of your arms?" Izzy wondered.

"I've already stretched my legs. I like to give my arms a stretch too," said Rory.

"Can I run with you?" Izzy requested.

"Of course you can. I was just going to do a little one today though because I ran quite far yesterday," Rory fibbed.

"Fuelled by pancakes," Izzy smiled.

"Sorry?" asked Rory.

"You know, the pancakes."

Rory looked at her blankly.

"The pancakes that you were about to have after you came to the pantry asking for some baking soda?"

"Oh thooooose pancakes. Yes, they were delicious, and kept me running for several miles. In fact, I ran for several miles and had so much energy left that I did the same loop again." He waited for a reaction from Izzy or a suggestion that he take it easy, but it never came. "And then I ran the loop again. Crazy how far I ran really."

"Are you ready then?" asked Izzy.

"Ready?" questioned Rory.

"Yes, to run!" she said, as she bounced into the forest.

Rory rolled his eyes into the back of his eye sockets and ran after her. Bobbee took great pleasure in watching the hilarity unfold.

"We'll just do a short one today, is that okay?" Rory suggested, as he puffed and panted trying to keep up with her.

He had the build of a runner but only liked the short and fast type of running, not the long-distance type. He preferred activities that used his mind and he thought that he had managed to dupe Izzy, but Izzy was full of beans and ran rings around him. She leapt about like a gazelle and he lagged behind. She could see that Rory was suffering, so she ran faster, and Rory ran faster to catch her until he was beyond exhausted.

"Time for the truth," Izzy demanded.

"The truth?" panicked Rory, as he tried to catch his breath.

"Yes. I know that you're up to something," she insisted as she ran a little faster.

"Not me," denied Rory as he tried to scrape the barrel of energy he didn't have.

"You want the straight facts?" she teased as she ran faster still. "You forgot that you ate pancakes, despite only having them yesterday. I saw you get into the back of Mr Zemmer's limousine yesterday morning before it drove away and then I saw you jump out of his helicopter yesterday afternoon. So, are you going to tell me what is going on?"

"I'm so sorry to ruin your super sleuthing,

but it wasn't me. I've been working on a school project in the forest," stated Rory, struggling to speak and run.

"Who are you kidding? Come on what's going on?" Izzy said as she kept running and running and running. Faster and faster and faster. Rory tried his hardest to keep up with her.

"Okay! Stop. Stop. Stop!" he yelled as he fell to his knees, exhausted. "We did get in the limousine."

"Rory!" hissed Bobbee.

"And we did get out of the helicopter, but I'm afraid that I can't tell you why. I'm sworn to secrecy."

"Phew," said Bobbee, relieved.

"We?" Izzy asked.

"Well, that was more than a slight overshare," declared Bobbee as he caught up with them.

"Slip of the tongue. It was just me," Rory said.

"Well, I did only see you so that makes sense," said Izzy.

"That was lucky," said Bobbee.

"I covered for you when your mum came looking for you, after you jumped in the back of the limousine. I told her that you just came to ask for baking soda for a project you were doing in the forest," Izzy said.

"Thank you," said Rory. "I owe you one."

"So, tell me why you were hugging that tree?" Izzy questioned, somewhat confused.

"I wanted to know how old it is to see if the forest can be protected. I'm worried that if Farmer Frank sells the land it will be cut down by developers," Rory shared.

"Were you hoping that it'd whisper its age into your ear if you hugged it?" Izzy laughed.

"Very funny..." Rory grumbled.

"I've got a better idea," Izzy suggested.

Rory watched from the rope swing as a small, lightly mud-spattered car arrived at Great Oaks, and a middle-aged woman stepped out. She immediately got out some paper and a measuring tape. Rory leapt from the seat and ran up to her like an excitable puppy.

"Are you from the local council?" Rory asked.

"I am indeed," the woman replied.

"Farmer Frank told me that the trees are one hundred and four feet tall and fifty feet around the trunk. Does that mean they can be protected for being ancient trees?" asked Rory.

"Maybe," said the council woman, not

giving anything away as she folded a piece of paper into a triangle and held it in between her eyes. Rory watched, fascinated, as she then walked backwards step by step. Rory mirrored her every step. Then she got out her measuring tape and measured from her toes to the base of the tree trunk. Then she scribbled a sum on another piece of paper. She then navigated the trunk of the tree using her measuring tape, calculating the full girth of the tree trunk.

"Well? Is it old?" asked Rory as he waited impatiently. "Can you tell its age?"

"Are you the young man who got in touch with us about a development contract?" she asked matter-of-factly.

"Yes, that was me. So?" he asked.

"Your farmer friend might have told his visitors a tall story about the size and age of the trees to try to impress *them*, but I'm afraid they just aren't ancient enough to be protected. I'm sorry that I can't help you. It's always such a shame to lose beautiful trees to development but there's nothing that I can do. Your best bet to save them is to prove that there are endangered or protected species living here," she said. "Then you'll have cause to announce the species presence to Natural England. Once they get involved, development will almost certainly be halted."

Chapter Ten

On the following morning, Rory stood dead still as he looked into the vastness that was Great Oaks Forest. Bobbee buzzed beside him.

"I have to be honest, I haven't got a clue where to start with this," said Rory, completely bewildered.

"Let's just start at the start," said Izzy, as she approached from behind, startling both Rory and Bobbee. "Pull up a comfy chair and we'll just make a note of every sight and every sound and hope that something protected crosses our path. And when it does, we'll take a picture of it as proof," she said.

"But what about the creatures that don't cross our path? There is no way that we can do all this by ourselves," moaned Rory as he sat down and kicked up the dirt, feeling sorry for himself once more. "We need an army of people to cover every inch of the forest. Why isn't anything ever simple?"

"The things worth having are never simple," said Bobbee as he rested his bee bottom on a beautiful daisy.

Rory looked into the distance in a sort of trance, trying to think of a solution.

"Oh no," said Rory with a resigned tone.

"Oh no?" questioned Izzy.

"I think I've found my army," said Rory.

"Well, what's 'oh no' about that? That's

great!" exclaimed Izzy. "Where?"

"Right there," said Rory, as he pointed to Travis and his friends, who were laying in the long grass aiming their paintball guns at a drink can balanced on a pile of stones.

"Okay. Good luck with that," said Bobbee.

Rory stood and took a deep breath, then began what felt like a hundred-mile trudge towards Travis and his gang. Bobbee buzzed beside him and Izzy watched from afar.

"Oh, hi Travis," Rory blurted out as he stood before them. "If you're bored, I could really do with some help."

Travis looked at him calmly at first, but when he recognised him he stood up, and charged towards Rory angrily.

"You what?" said Travis aggressively as he grabbed Rory by his collar, narrowly missing Bobbee. "How about my fist in your face? Do you need help with that?"

"How about you use your keen eye to look at nature instead of paintball targets? I'm doing a census of the wildlife within the forest, but I can't do it on my own. So, I wondered, if you were bored, whether you might be able to help me?" he stuttered. "Unless you're scared of the wildlife?"

"I ain't scared of nothing," growled Travis as he pulled Rory by the collar towards his face.

"That's good. I was afraid of squirrels. And birds, and cats, and just about everything really. But I'm not anymore," said Rory.

"Why should I care?" said Travis.

"If this forest is sold, then a developer will wipe it out with bulldozers, which will mean that the trees and the animals that live within it will die, and the entire area will be stripped of its livelihood. I need to prove that there is a protected species living here to stand a chance of saving it. And I need to prove it now! Everyone should care about nature. It's our life source."

"Well, I don't care, so run along," he said dismissively, as he pushed Rory back in the direction he had come from. Rory stumbled but managed to stay on his feet as he straightened his collar and returned to Izzy.

"Don't worry. We'll just do what we can, and that will have to be good enough," said Bobbee.

"It's pointless. You may as well call Queen Bee now and tell her that she chose the wrong kid for this mission, and that I'm sorry I let her down."

"Oi, ginger kid!" said a voice from behind.

Rory turned to see one of Travis' allies standing there. "My *name* is Rory," he said with strength.

"Sorry, Rory. I want to help," said the boy.

"You do?" said Rory, somewhat surprised and completely lost for words.

"If I can?" he asked.

"Of course! I'll explain what we need to do," said Rory.

"I'd like to help too," said another voice.

"Me too," said another.

Rory looked around to see all of Travis' allies in a long eager line. Suddenly, Travis burst through the middle of them, pushing them out of his way.

"Traitors, the lot of you," he said.

"I'm not a traitor. I'd quite like this forest to always be here," said one of them.

"I knew that there had to be more to life than shooting paintball pellets and turns out that there is!" said another.

"Can we enlist your help too?" Rory asked Travis, with a sort of new spring in his step.

Travis looked around at his former allies.

"Fine," agreed Travis miserably.

"My grandson, the secret agent," whispered Bobbee with a nudge and a wink, super proud.

"Excellent," exclaimed Rory. "So, this is the plan. We will split the forest up into rows and columns. Each of us is then responsible for the census of creatures within five trees squared." Travis said nothing, but nodded a single agreeable nod. "Great. So, everyone come and take a piece of paper from my notepad and—"

"Everyone has a phone. We'll just write our notes in there. It will save the paper," said Travis.

"Great idea," said Rory. "Are we all ready to go then?" Rory asked the crowd. They all nodded. "Then let's do it," Rory charged forward as if he were heading for war, and he led the children into the trees and then watched as the sea of welly boots scattered in different directions.

Deep inside the forest, Rory pulled up a garden chair, rested a piece of paper on his knee and watched and waited. A beautiful jay flew overhead and landed in the trees. Rory marked it down. A ladybird rested on a bluebell. He marked it down. A group of deer stopped for a snack of luscious green grass and were scared off by Farmer Frank's dog. He marked them down. He felt like he was at a sight test at the opticians as creatures popped in and out of his peripheral vision and he had to mark every spot.

Izzy pulled up a garden chair next to Rory.

"What have you seen?" she asked.

Rory relayed his creature count so far. "And you?" Rory asked.

"Nothing unusual or unexpected. I'm almost

certain that I've seen a red squirrel in this forest before though. It was during my last visit. I'm sure of it."

"That would be perfect if someone could prove that a red squirrel lived here. I'll go and check on everyone and see what we have noted," said Rory, getting up from his chair and walking into the woods.

Two hours later, he returned to his garden chair next to Izzy, looking glum.

"Your face says that we haven't found what we wanted," said Izzy.

"No. We've seen some amazing creatures, but nothing that ticks the protected species box. I was sure that we could locate some evidence of bats, or badgers, or even red squirrels, but nobody has, and we are almost out of time."

Chapter Eleven

Rory opened his eyes to a deep rumbling sound that made his toes tremble. Lying in bed, awaiting his alarm, he pulled back his cover and peeked out from behind his curtain. He saw that not one but *three* bulldozers had rolled into the campsite and had gathered outside Farmer Frank's house. The limousine followed behind like a black cloud. Mr Zemmer got out and knocked on the front door.

"Come on Frank, it's time to go now.

Nobody wants any upset, so out you come."

There was no movement from the house. Rory saw a curtain twitch at the side of the house, and immediately after the twitch, Izzy appeared and looked straight at Rory with concern written all over her face.

"Please help!" she mouthed to him. Rory pulled his coat on over his pyjamas, opened the door and ran out of the caravan towards the farmhouse.

"You can't do this," yelled Rory to Mr Zemmer.

"I'm afraid that I can young man," said Mr Zemmer arrogantly.

Rory pulled out the piece of paper that he had marked for the wildlife census and waved it around above his head.

"This piece of paper proves that there is protected wildlife in this forest, which means that you and your bulldozers are trespassing on protected property," he bluffed.

"Says who?" said Mr Zemmer, concerned for his deal.

"The Conservation of Habitats and Species Regulations, 2010," said Rory convincingly.

"Let me see that," said Mr Zemmer as he lurched at Rory.

"Rory run!" yelled Izzy as she appeared at the front door.

Rory ran as fast as he could into the forest. Mr Zemmer watched him and jumped into the passenger seat of the limousine.

"Follow that child," he said to the chauffeur, who put his foot on the accelerator and drove towards the forest.

"Run away from the forest, not into it." yelled Bobbee as he buzzed beside Rory.

Rory ran away from the forest and towards the farm. The limousine was in hot pursuit as it bumped up and down on the old dirt tracks of the tractors, and the driver and Mr Zemmer bumped up and down inside, hitting their heads on the windows and the roof of the limousine. Suddenly, a red squirrel appeared from nowhere and ran in front of it. The limousine lost control and drove head first into the dung heap next to the cow shed. Rory turned to see the devastation and there, beneath the car, was a red squirrel, flat on its back.

"Is it going to be okay?" asked Rory.

"I hope so," replied Bobbee as he buzzed over it. The squirrel opened its eyes wearily and started to make a sort of quiet squeak. Bobbee leant in.

"Do you understand squirrel?" asked Rory.

"No, but the queen gave me this," he said as he pulled out another gadget from his bee backpack. "It is an app that translates from wildlife to English. Let me see if I can work it.

What did you say?" Bobbee asked the squirrel. The squirrel squeaked again, and Bobbee frowned as he looked at his translation app, trying to decipher the code. "He is saying red, red, red. I think." Bobbee looked at the squirrel. "Yes, we know you're red. We are so happy that you are red, too." The squirrel squeaked again and Bobbee translated.

"No, my wife is called Red," said the squirrel.

"You have a wife?" asked Bobbee. "That's wonderful. There are more red squirrels in our forest Rory. Where is your wife?" asked Bobbee. Immediately the squirrel's eyes closed.

"No, no, no, no," said Rory. "We have to wake him up, Grandad. I need to find his family and take a photo to prove that Great Oaks should be saved."

"How do we wake him?" asked Bobbee.

"We can give him some honey!" said Rory excitedly pulling out the jar from his toolkit. He held it up to his face which magnified his eye, but his excited stare soon drooped when he saw the empty jar. "Oh no!" he whined as he unscrewed the lid and turned the jar upside down to confirm that there was in fact none left. Not even a dribble. But just as he screwed the lid back on he felt a sort of crunching where the honey had crystalised around the rim.

"Oh, please, please, please," he said, as he used a fingernail to remove some of the honey crystals.

Bobbee climbed onto the squirrel's snout and used his feet to push the squirrel's top and bottom jaw apart so that Rory could drop some honey crystals inside. Then they sat back and waited. And waited.

"This is so unfair," cried Rory in frustration. "We were about to find out where the squirrel's wife—"

"Squeak, squeak, squeak, squeak," said the squirrel, in a sort of muffled way because Bobbee was yet to stop being a muzzle on his jaw.

Bobbee buzzed away and checked his app whilst the squirrel sat up on his hind legs as he came around slowly. "He says that he and his wife have been hiding in an abandoned rabbit's warren where they had stored acorns from last year, before the pink fungus arrived and destroyed all of their food, and their home. She is pregnant with their first baby," Bobbee revealed.

"That's amazing! We need to get the squirrel and his pregnant wife back to their comfortable nest away from predators and get photographic evidence to submit to

Natural England so that Mr Zemmer will leave Great Oaks alone once and for all," Rory exclaimed.

Bobbee buzzed into his app so that he could relay this to the squirrel, and he was only too pleased to help. The squirrel stood onto all four legs, alert once more, and rushed into the forest with Rory and Bobbee hot in pursuit.

Izzy held Farmer Frank's hand as they all gathered around the bent-up limousine, which was surrounded in steaming dung. Rory thrust the photograph of the happy red squirrel family into the hands of Mr Zemmer, who was still in a daze in the back of the limousine with the car airbag deployed in front of him.

"You see. A protected species lives at Great Oaks, and therefore your contract of sale is null and void. I have also emailed this proof to Natural England so there is no point in contesting it. I suggest that you send your bulldozers away before we call the police for trespassing."

Mr Zemmer took one look of the photograph of the red squirrel family and headbutted his airbag.

Farmer Frank took the contract from out of his back pocket and hurled it onto the dung heap. "That's where that belongs then," he laughed. "Your Grandad would've been so proud of you Rory, well done."

"Thank you, Farmer Frank. I'm sure that he is looking down on us and enjoying the moment too," he said, as he looked in Bobbee's direction with a knowing smile.

"You bet I am," said Bobbee with a wink. "A right chip off the old block, aren't you?" he said playfully.

Chapter Twelve

Dad started to put the suitcases into the boot of the car whilst Mum secured Lucy into her car seat. She was sad to be leaving, but she had a very strong feeling that her dad Bobbee was still close. She smiled to herself and then looked around to find Rory.

"Rory?" she called. "It's time to go."

Rory was still packing up the last of his things whilst Bobbee sat on the window ledge watching him. A shiny red sports car pulled into the driveway.

"Looks like Farmer Frank has a new problem," he said.

"You're kidding?" said Rory, as he got close to the window and looked out.

He gathered his remaining clothes and screwed them up, shoving them into his bag in a hurry. Bobbee buzzed onto the bag as Rory tossed it over his shoulder at speed whilst running out of the caravan. Rory chucked the bag into the car boot, completely ignoring his mum, and ran towards the farmhouse with Bobbee in pursuit.

"Slow down speedy," Bobbee fussed.

"Where are you going?" Mum shouted after him. "We need to be home in time to get you ready for school tomorrow."

"I won't be long, I promise," yelled Rory as he ran.

"And how many times have I heard that?" said his mum under her breath.

Rory hid along the pathway next to the farmhouse and watched as a short, well-dressed lady stepped out of the drivers' side door.

"That's the investor from Mr Zemmer's meeting," Rory whispered to Bobbee, who sat on a rose next to Rory's face. "Here we go again."

The lady walked to the front door of the farmhouse and knocked loudly. Farmer Frank opened it.

"Frank, is it?" she asked.

"That's correct. What can I do for you?" he asked.

"I have a proposal for you," she said.

"Great Oaks is no longer for sale, madam, so you've had a wasted journey I'm afraid," he said proudly, as he tried to close the door.

"No, no, it's not that kind of proposal," she said. "You see, my son helped with a wildlife census here a couple of days ago and it's all that he has spoken about since. Quite honestly, I've never seen him so engaged with anything before. It's like he is a completely different child." The investor opened up the rear passenger door, revealing Travis sitting on the backseat.

"Travis is your son?" Rory blurted out, making everyone aware of his presence.

"Yes. And he speaks very highly of you, Rory," she said. "It got me thinking. I believe that you could have something very special here to offer school educators," she explained.

"In what way?" asked Farmer Frank, intrigued.

"By offering some sort of residential program on-site, to teach young people about the importance of conservation."

Rory was feeling unsure.

"Check this out, Rory," said Travis as he jumped out of the car, holding a jar containing a germinating acorn. "Isn't it amazing?"

Rory looked at it in awe.

"It really is," said Rory, as he looked at Farmer Frank. "I mean, you could do with a little financial and creative help couldn't you Farmer Frank?"

"And I know the headteacher of Travis' school," she said excitedly. "We can start there."

Farmer Frank smiled at her. "It sounds like a great place to start, Mrs...?"

"You can call me Elodie," she said, reaching out a hand.

"Rory!" called Mum.

"I have to go," said Rory. "But this all sounds very exciting."

Izzy appeared behind her grandfather. "It really does," she said. "Thank you, Rory."

"What for?" he asked

"For being you," she said with a smile.

Rory's face glowed red with embarrassment as he turned on his heels and waved to them all awkwardly. He walked away towards his mum and dad, who were waiting impatiently by the car for him.

"Just one more thing," said Rory, as he sprinted past them. They threw up their arms in despair.

Rory and Bobbee stood facing each other in a clearing in the forest.

"You smashed it kid," said Bobbee as he charged at Rory's upper arm in a sort of buddy punch.

Immediately, Queen Bee appeared and

settled on Rory's nose, which made him cross-eyed. "Mission complete, I'd say. Jolly well done," she said, and she presented him with a tiny medal which she attached to his shirt collar. "You are a true secret agent now."

"Thank you, Your Majesty," he said.

"And this is for you," she said, as she presented Bobbee with a medal and attached it to his fuzzy black and gold body. Bobbee saluted her, proud as punch. "Really great work both of you," she said as she buzzed off.

"Time to go then," said Bobbee.

"But I don't want you to go," said Rory, upset.

"I'm not going anywhere kid, not without you, not now, not ever. I meant time to go home," said Bobbee. Rory grabbed hold of him and squeezed him in tightly to his cheek.

"Thank goodness," said Rory.

They turned and headed back to the car, slowly, not wanting to leave.

"You'd better make a home for me in your Lego Batcave or something," said Bobbee.

"I am sure that I can come up with something more comfortable than that for my favourite Grandad in the whole world," Rory smiled.

Acknowledgments

Thank you to Hannah Farrant at Felt Things (@felt.things) for your amazing needle felting talents, bringing Rory & Bobbee to life in felt form, and Dan Fishman at Dan Fish Photography (@danfishphoto) for translating that beautifully into an image to adorn the cover of this book. Thank you also to Greg Carter (@greg_carter_visual_artist) for his wonderful illustrations and a special mention to Lily Chambers who has tirelessly injected her amazing doodle energy into the Rory

Green Instagram Campaign. Thank you all!

If you would like to keep up to date with Rory and his adventures, head over to my website kerrymcintosh.co.uk or follow @kmcintoshwrites on Instagram!

BV - #0012 - 220224 - C0 - 197/132/9 - PB - 9781803780573 - Gloss Lamination